Smitten
with
Kittens

and all the cute things
that kittens will DO?

Like eat a big breakfast,

then wash up and . . .

POSE!

And chase butterflies
till one lands on their . . .

NOSE!

They look in the mirror
and think, *Who is THAT?*

Looking right back

s a very fierce CAT!

Kittens make trouble
whatever they DO—
rolling, more rolling . . .

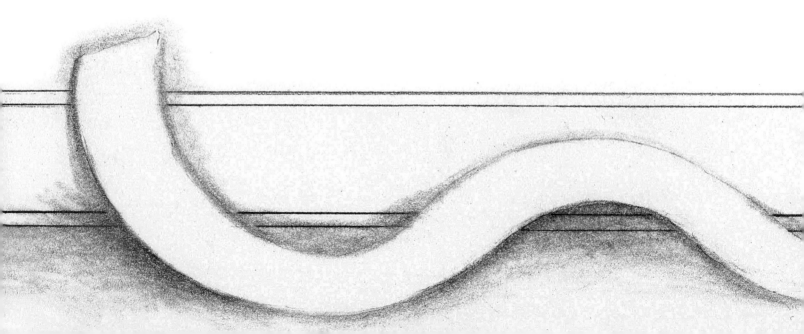

and out the door,
TOO!

Kittens love watching
their most favorite SHOW.

Birds flit and flutter.
Where did those birds GO?

Kittens like hiding
in tight, little SPACES.

Sometimes they're found in the silliest PLACES.

A kitten's day is filled with play,
and now it's time to take a . . .

NAP.

Fun and mischief
fill their dreams . . .

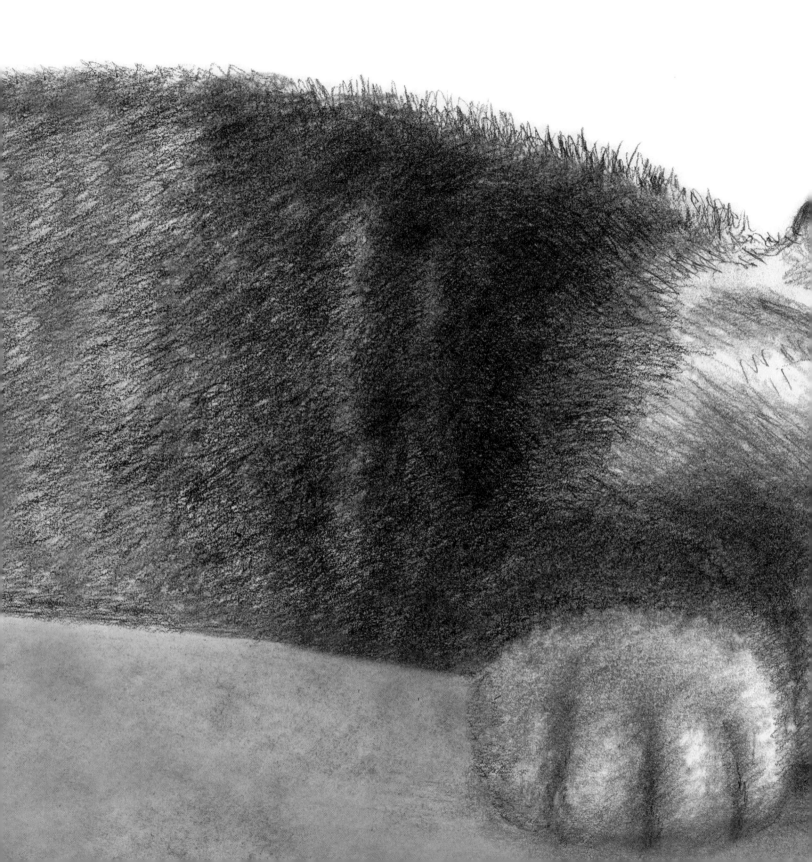

all curled up in a cozy LAP.

Fun Facts

1. Gently pet and cuddle kittens every day so they get used to being touched, especially around their tail and paws. Talk to them, too, so they learn the sound of your voice. This might make it easier when you need to clip their nails!

2. All kittens are born with blue eyes. Some breeds, like Siamese, Ragdoll, and Tonkinese, keep their blue color. Most other breeds shift to their permanent eye color within a year.

3. Kittens are born deaf, but by the time they are four weeks old, they can hear three times better than humans. A human ear has two muscles, but a cat's ear has thirty-two.

4. Are you a righty or a lefty? Kittens can be right-pawed and left-pawed, too!

5. Kittens sleep about eighteen hours a day. This gives them the energy they need for growing into strong, healthy adult cats.

6. Kittens and cats have excellent smell and hearing, but their vision is not as sharp. Their whiskers help them sense the world around them, acting a bit like radar detectors. Whiskers should never be cut.

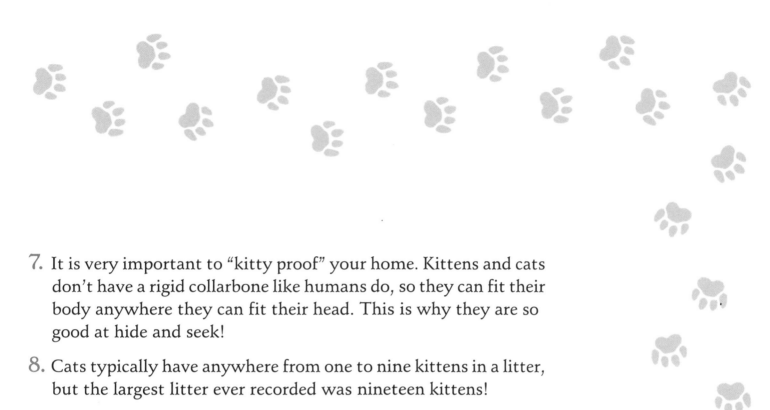

7. It is very important to "kitty proof" your home. Kittens and cats don't have a rigid collarbone like humans do, so they can fit their body anywhere they can fit their head. This is why they are so good at hide and seek!

8. Cats typically have anywhere from one to nine kittens in a litter, but the largest litter ever recorded was nineteen kittens!

9. When kittens or grown-up cats blink slowly at you, they are letting you know they feel safe and comfortable and are showing you affection. Some people call this a kitty kiss. Cats also blink slowly at other cats.

10. Train kittens to feel safe and comfortable in their cat carrier by placing treats and a soft towel inside. Try leaving the carrier open for them to sleep in, too. This can be a big help when it is time for them to travel to the vet or go on vacation.

In loving memory of Miss Kitty, Mouse, Willie, and Sofie, and for Cindercat. Thank you for all the joy and laughter.—F. M.

To Florence.—W. M.

Published by Charlesbridge
9 Galen Street
Watertown, MA 02472
(617) 926-0329 • www.charlesbridge.com

Library of Congress Cataloging-in-Publication Data
Names: Minor, Florence Friedmann, author. | Minor, Wendell, illustrator.
Title: Smitten with kittens / Florence Minor; illustrated by Wendell Minor.
Description: Watertown, MA: Charlesbridge, [2022] | Audience: Ages 3–7. |
   Audience: Grades K–1. | Summary: "Celebrate all the things that kittens
   do as they play, explore, and make mischief."—Provided by publisher.
Identifiers: LCCN 2020051074 (print) | LCCN 2020051075 (ebook)
   | ISBN 9781623541675 (hardcover) | ISBN 9781632899651 (ebook)
Subjects: LCSH: Kittens—Juvenile fiction. | Kittens—Juvenile poetry. Stories in
   rhyme. | Picture books for children. | CYAC: Stories in rhyme. | Cats—Fiction.
   | Animals—Infancy—Fiction. | LCGFT: Stories in rhyme. | Picture books.
Classification: LCC PZ8.3.M6465 Sm 2022 (print) | LCC PZ8.3.M6465 (ebook)
   | DDC [E]—dc23
LC record available at https://lccn.loc.gov/2020051074
LC ebook record available at https://lccn.loc.gov/2020051075

Printed in China
(hc) 10 9 8 7 6 5 4 3 2 1

Illustrations done in graphite on paper and digital
Display type set in Edwardian by Elsner+Flake Designstudios
Text type set in Schneidler by Bitstream Inc.
Color separations and printing by 1010 Printing International Limited in
   Huizhou, Guangdong, China
Production supervision by Jennifer Most Delaney
Designed by Diane M. Earley